Carol of the Cobblers

Bring the Christmas in—
Bring the Christmas in.
Tap and peg and sew the leather
Strong for winter's harshest weather.

Bring the Christmas in—
Bring the Christmas in.
Stop all work and light the candles;
Reverently put out His sandals.

Bring the Christmas in—
Bring the Christmas in.
Bring in the Child. While we are waiting
Purge us clean of sin and hating.

Bring the Christmas in—
Bring the Christmas in.
Hush, His steps, mayhap He's coming;
Make for Him a blithesome homing.

Bring the Christmas in—
Bring the Christmas in.
Carol clear, casting all fear out.
May His sandals wear the year out.
Bring the Christmas in—
Bring the Christmas in.

Once upon a time....

The
Remarkable Christmas
of the
Cobbler's Sons

Told by Ruth Sawyer

Pictures by Barbara Cooney

Viking

nce upon a time, in the snowcapped mountains
of the Tirol, there lived the king of all the goblins. His name
was Laurin, King Laurin. His kingdom was under the earth,
and all the gold and silver of the mountains belonged to him.
But his greatest treasure was his lovely daughter. She was
very unlike her squat, little father. With his bulbous nose and
big ears he looked as old as the mountains.

King Laurin's daughter loved flowers, and often she was sad because none grew in her father's kingdom.

"I want a garden of roses, roses like the sunrise and the sunset," she told her father. And the king laughed.

"You shall have such a garden," said he. "I will have it roofed with crystal so that the sun will pour into the depths of the kingdom and make the flowers grow lovely and fragrant." And this he did.

Every evening when the sun set, the color of the goblin princess's rose garden spread upward on the mountains, so that the snow caught it and the people in the valley pointed in wonder to their rose-glowing Alps. Ever after they spoke of the color as alpenglow.

King Laurin was merry and gay and loved to play pranks. Sometimes he would visit the valleys where people lived or pop into a herdsman's hut halfway up the mountain.

There are many tales about King Laurin. This is one that Tirolese mothers tell their children.

Long ago there lived in one of the valleys a very poor cobbler indeed. His wife had died and left him with three children, little boys, all of them—Fritzl, Franzl, and Hansl. They lived in a hut so small there was only one room in it, and in that was the cobbler's bench, a hearth for cooking, a stove for warmth, and a big bed full of straw. On the wall were racks for a few dishes. A bench ran around two walls, and, of course, there was a table with chairs. They needed few dishes or pans, for there was never much to cook or eat. Sometimes the cobbler would mend the Sunday shoes of a farmer, and then there was good goat's milk to drink. Sometimes he would mend the holiday shoes of the baker, and then there was the good, long crusty loaf of bread to eat. And sometimes he mended the shoes of the butcher, and then there was the good stew, cooked with meat in the pot, and noodles, leeks, and herbs.

When the cobbler gathered the little boys around the table and they had said their grace, he would laugh and clap his hands and sometimes even dance. "Ha-ha!" he would shout. "Today we have the good . . . what? Ah-h . . . today we eat . . . Schnitzle, Schnotzle, and Schnootzle!"

With that he would swing the kettle off the hook and fill every bowl brimming full, and Fritzl, Franzl, and Hansl would eat until they had had enough. Ach, those were the good days—the days of having Schnitzle, Schnotzle, and Schnootzle. Of course, the cobbler was making up nonsense and nothing else, but the stew tasted so much better because of the nonsense.

Now a year came, with every month following his brother
on leaden feet. The little boys and the cobbler heard the month of
March tramp out and April tramp in. They heard June tramp out and
July tramp in. And every month marched heavier than his brother.
And that was because war was among them again. War, with workers
taking up their guns and leaving mothers and children to care for
themselves as best they could; and there was scant to pay even
a poor cobbler for mending shoes. The whole village shuffled
to church with the soles flapping and the heels lopsided, and
the eyelets and buttons and straps quite gone.

Summer—that was not so bad. But winter came and covered up the good earth, and gone were the roots, the berries, the sorrel, and the corn. The tramp of November going out and December coming in was very loud indeed.

As Christmas grew near, the little boys began to wonder if there would be any feast for them, if there would be the good father dancing about the room and laughing "Ha-ha," and singing "Ho-ho," and saying: "Now, this being Christmas Day we have the good . . . what?" And this time the little boys knew that they would never wait for their father to say it; they would shout themselves: "We know—it is the good Schnitzle, Schnotzle, and Schnootzle!" Ach, how very long it was since their father had mended shoes for the butcher! Surely—surely—there would be need soon again, with Christmas so near.

At last came the Eve of Christmas. The little boys climbed along the beginnings of the Brenner-Alp, looking for fagots. The trees had shed so little that year; every branch was green and grew fast to its tree, so little was there of dead, dried brush to fill their arms and baskets.

When they had a small fire started, their father came in, slapping his arms about his body, trying to put warmth back into it. "Good news!" he said. "The soldiers are marching into the village. They will have boots that need mending, those soldiers." He pinched a cheek of each little boy. "You shall see—tonight I will come home with . . . what?"

"Schnitzle, Schnotzle, and Schnootzle," they shouted.

So happy they were they forgot there was nothing to eat for supper—not a crust, not a slice of cold porridge-pudding. "Will the soldiers have money to pay you?" asked Fritzl, the oldest.

"Not the soldiers, perhaps, but the captains. There might even be a general. I will mend the boots of the soldiers for nothing, for after all what day is coming tomorrow! They fight for us, those soldiers; we mend for them, ja? But a general—he will have plenty of money."

The boys helped their father put all his tools, all his pieces of leather into his pack; he wound and wound and wound the woolen scarf about his neck, while he pulled the cap far down on his head. "It will be a night to freeze the ears off you," he said. "Now bolt the door after me, keep the fire burning with a little at a time; and climb into bed and pull the quilt over you. And let no one in!"

He was gone. They bolted the door; they put a little on the fire; they climbed into the big bed, putting Hansl, the smallest, in the middle. They pulled up the quilt, such a thin quilt to keep out so much cold! Straight and still and close together they lay, looking up at the little spot of light the fire made on the ceiling, watching their breath go upward in icy spurts. With the going of the sun the wind rose. First it whispered: it whispered of good fires in big chimneys; it whispered of the pines on the mountainsides; it whispered of snow loosening and sliding over the glaciers. Then it began to blow: it blew hard, it blew quarrelsome, it blew cold and colder. And at last it roared. It roared its wintry breath through the cracks in the walls and under the door. And Fritzl, Franzl, and Hansl drew closer together and shivered.

Whee . . . ooh . . . bang, bang!

Whee . . . ooh . . . bang, bang!

"Is it the wind or someone knocking?" asked Franzl.

"It is the wind," said Fritzl.

Whee . . . ooh . . . knock, knock!

"Is it the wind or someone knocking?" asked Hansl.

"It is the wind *and* someone knocking!" said Fritzl.

He rolled out of the bed and went to the window. It looked out directly on the path to the door. "Remember what our father said: do not open it," said Franzl.

But Fritzl looked and looked. Close to the hut, beaten against it by the wind, stood a little man. He was pounding on the door. Now they could hear him calling: "Let me in! I tell you, let me in!"

"Oh, don't, don't!" cried Hansl.

"I must," said Fritzl. "He looks very cold. The wind is tearing at him as a wolf tears at a young lamb"; and with that he drew the bolt and into the hut skipped the oddest little man they had ever seen. He had a great peaked cap tied onto his head with deer-thongs. He had a round red face out of which stuck a bulbous nose, like a fat plum on a pudding. He had big ears. And his teeth were chattering so hard they made the chairs to dance. He shook his fist at the three little boys. "Ach, kept me waiting. Wanted to keep all the good food, all the good fire to yourselves? Na-na, that is no kind of hospitality."

He looked over at the little bit of a fire on the hearth, making hardly any heat in the hut. He looked at the empty table, not a bowl set or a spoon beside it. He took up the big pot, peered into it, turned it upside down to make sure nothing was clinging to the bottom, set it down with a bang. "So—you have already eaten it all. Greedy boys. But if you have saved no feast for me, you can at least warm me." With that he climbed into the big straw-bed with Franzl and Hansl, with his cap still tied under his chin. Fritzl tried to explain that they had not been greedy, that there had never been any food, not for days, to speak of. But he was too frightened of the little man, of his eyes as sharp and blue as ice, of his mouth so grumbling.

"Roll over, roll over," the little man was shouting at the two in the bed. "I have no room! Roll over and give me my half of the quilt."

Fritzl saw that he was pushing his brothers out of the bed. "Na-na," he said, trying to make peace with their guest. "They are little, those two. There is room for all if we but lie quiet." And he started to climb into the bed himself.

But the little man bounced and rolled about shouting: "Give me room, give me more quilt. Can't you see I'm cold? I call this poor hospitality to bring a stranger inside your door, give him nothing to eat, and then grudge him bed and covering to keep him warm." He dug his elbow into the side of skinny little Hansl.

Fritzl began to feel angry. "Sir," he said, "I pray you to be gentle with my little brother. I am sorry there is nothing to give you. But our father, the cobbler, has gone to mend shoes for the soldiers. When he returns we look for food. Truly, this is a night to feast and to share. If you will but lie still until he comes I promise you . . ."

The little man rolled over and stuck his elbow into Fritzl's ribs. "Promise—promise. Na-na, what good is a promise? Come get out of bed and give me your place." He drew up his knees, put his feet in the middle of Fritzl's back, and pushed with a great strength. The next moment the boy was spinning across the room.

"There you go," roared the little man after him. "If you must keep warm, turn cartwheels, turn them fast."

For a moment Fritzl stood sullenly by the small speck of fire. He felt bruised and very angry. He looked over at the bed. Sure enough, the greedy little man had rolled himself up in the quilt, leaving only a short corner of it for the two younger boys. He had taken more than half of the straw for himself, and was even then pushing and digging at Hansl.

Brrr . . . it was cold! Before he knew it Fritzl was doing as he had been told, turning cartwheels around the room. He had passed the table and was coming toward the bed when—plop! Plop—plop—plop! Things were falling out of his pockets every time his feet swung high over his head. Plop—plop—plop! The two younger boys were sitting up in bed. It was their cries of astonishment which brought Fritzl's feet back to the floor again, to stay. In a circle about the room, he had left behind him a golden trail of oranges. Such oranges—big as two fists! And sprinkled everywhere between were comfits wrapped in gold and silver paper. Fritzl stood and gaped at them.

"Here, you, get out and keep warm yourself!" shouted the little man as he dug Franzl in the ribs. "Cartwheels for you, boy!" And the next minute Franzl was whirling in cartwheels about the room. Plop— plop—plop! Things were dropping out of his pockets: Christmas buns, Christmas cookies covered with icing, with plums, with anise and caraway seeds.

The little man was digging Hansl now in the ribs. "Lazy boy, greedy boy. Think you can have the bed to yourself now? Na-na, I'll have it! Out you go!" And he put his feet against the littlest boy's back and pushed him onto the floor. "Cartwheels . . ." he began; but Fritzl, forgetting his amazement at what was happening, shouted: "But, sir, he is too little. He cannot turn . . ."

"Hold him up in the corner, then. You keep warmer when your heels are higher than your head. Step lively there. Take a leg, each of you, and be quick about it."

So angry did the little man seem, so fiery and determined, that Fritzl and Franzl hurried their little brother over to the corner, stood him on his head, and each held a leg. Donner and Blitzen! What happened then! Whack— whack—whickety-whack! Whack— whack—whickety-whack! Pelting the floor like hail against the roof came silver and gold pieces, all pouring out of Hansl's pockets.

Fritzl began to shout, Franzl began to dance. Hansl began to shout: "Let me down, let me down!" When they did the three little boys danced around the pile, taking hands, singing "Tra-la-la," and "Fiddle-de-dee," and "Ting-a-ling-a-ling," until their breath was gone and they could dance no longer. They looked over at the bed and Fritzl was opening his mouth to say: "Now, if you please, sir, we can offer you some Christmas cheer . . ." But the bed was empty, the quilt lay in a heap on the floor. The little man had gone.

The three little boys were gathering up the things on the floor—putting oranges into the big wooden bowl, buns and cookies onto the two platters, silver and gold pieces into this dish and that. And right in the midst of it in came their father, stamping and puffing. He had brought bread, he had brought milk, meat for the good stew—and noodles.

Such a wonder, such a clapping of hands, such a singing as they worked to get ready the Christmas feast! Fritzl began the story about their Christmas guest; Franzl told it mid-through; but little Hansl finished, making his brothers stand him on his head again to show just how it was that all the silver and gold had tumbled out of his pockets.

"We are the lucky ones," said the cobbler. "Always I thought it was just a tale the grandfathers told the children. The saying goes that King Laurin comes every year at the Christmas to one hut—one family—to play his tricks and share his treasure horde."

"He was a very ugly little man," said Hansl. "He dug us in our ribs and took all the bed for himself."

"That was the king—that is the way he plays at being fierce. Say the blessing: 'Come, Little Jesus, and be our guest,' then draw up the chairs. Ah-h . . . what have we to eat?"

The little boys shouted the answer all together: "Schnitzle—Schnotzle—and Schnootzle!"

For three friends: Matthew, Mark, and Brett
—B.C.

VIKING
Published by the Penguin Group
Penguin Books USA Inc., 375 Hudson Street, New York, New York 10014, U.S.A.
Penguin Books Ltd, 27 Wrights Lane, London W8 5TZ, England
Penguin Books Australia Ltd, Ringwood, Victoria, Australia
Penguin Books Canada Ltd, 10 Alcorn Avenue, Toronto, Ontario, Canada M4V 3B2
Penguin Books (N.Z.) Ltd, 182-190 Wairau Road, Auckland 10, New Zealand

Penguin Books Ltd, Registered Offices: Harmondsworth, Middlesex, England

First published in 1994 by Viking, a division of Penguin Books USA Inc.

1 3 5 7 9 10 8 6 4 2

Text copyright Ruth Sawyer, 1941   Copyright renewed Ruth Sawyer, 1969
Illustrations copyright © Barbara Cooney, 1994
All rights reserved
"The Remarkable Christmas of the Cobbler's Sons," under the title "Schnitzle, Schnotzle, and Schnootzle,"
was originally published in *The Long Christmas* by Ruth Sawyer, The Viking Press, 1941.

LIBRARY OF CONGRESS CATALOGING-IN-PUBLICATION DATA
Sawyer, Ruth, 1880–1970.   The remarkable Christmas of the cobbler's sons /
told by Ruth Sawyer; painted by Barbara Cooney.   p.   cm.
Summary: A poor cobbler and his three sons worry about having food for
their Christmas feast, until a playful goblin king pays them a visit.
ISBN 0-670-84922-7
[1. Folklore—Austria. 2. Christmas—Folklore.] I. Cooney, Barbara, ill. II. Title.
PZ8.1.S262Re 1994 [398.2]—dc20 —dc20 [398.2'0943602] 94-10934 CIP AC

Printed in U.S.A.   Set in Sabon